Cars! Cars! And More Cars!

Paper Plate Cars

These cars are cute as a bug! To make the wheels, trace around a jar lid on a piece of construction paper and cut out two circles. Attach the wheels to half of a paper plate as shown. Add details to the car with crayons, markers, or paint.

Make Tire Tracks

Here's a fun way to paint! Have your child finger paint a large piece of finger-paint paper or shelf-liner paper. Set the painting aside to dry. When the paint has dried, complete the picture. Let your child roll wheels of a toy car over a washable black ink pad and then drive the car over the dry paint to make tire tracks.

There are Many Ways to Travel

(tune: "She'll Be Comin' Round The Mountain")

There are many ways to travel here and there.
There are many ways to travel here and there.
You can travel in a car,
If you're traveling near or far.
There are many ways to travel here and there.

Design a License Plate

Encourage your child to create a license plate from a shoe box lid. The license plate could have random letters or numbers, or be personalized with your child's name or a cute saying. If your child is not yet ready to print, he/she could use letter or number sponges to make prints on the box lid. Your child could also cut large letters or numbers from magazines or newspapers, and glue the letters or numbers to the lid. The child could also dictate information for you to print on the lid. Then your child could squeeze glue along the letters or numbers and arrange collage materials in the glue. Just for fun, attach the finished license plate to a riding toy.

Cars! Cars!

Steering Wheels

Cut out the center from a large paper plate and save the rim. Let your child pretend the rim is a steering wheel and "drive" around the backyard or playground. Beep! Beep! Here comes the car!

Drive a Car

With just a little imagination, a grocery store box can become a car or truck! Cut the top off, attach paper plate wheels to the sides, and draw other details with crayons or markers to make the box resemble a car. Your child will have a carload of fun sitting in the box pretending to drive!

How Wheels Help Us!

Conduct a simple experiment to show how wheels can help us. Gather a pile of blocks. Encourage your child to experiment with different ways to move the blocks. After he/she has tried several ways to transport the blocks, suggest using a wagon to move the blocks. Discuss which was the easiest way and which was the most difficult.

Park Cars

Here's a fun way to help your child compare sizes. Collect four to five sizes of toy cars and a box for each size. Take the tops off the boxes and cut an opening in one side of each box to make a garage door. Turn each box upside down so it resembles a garage with a roof. As your child parks the cars in the garages, discuss which garage is the best choice for each car.

Dashboard Prop

Glue dashboard to a cereal box. Attach a small paper plate where indicated with yarn. (Older children may use a brass fastener.) Use the plate as a steering wheel.

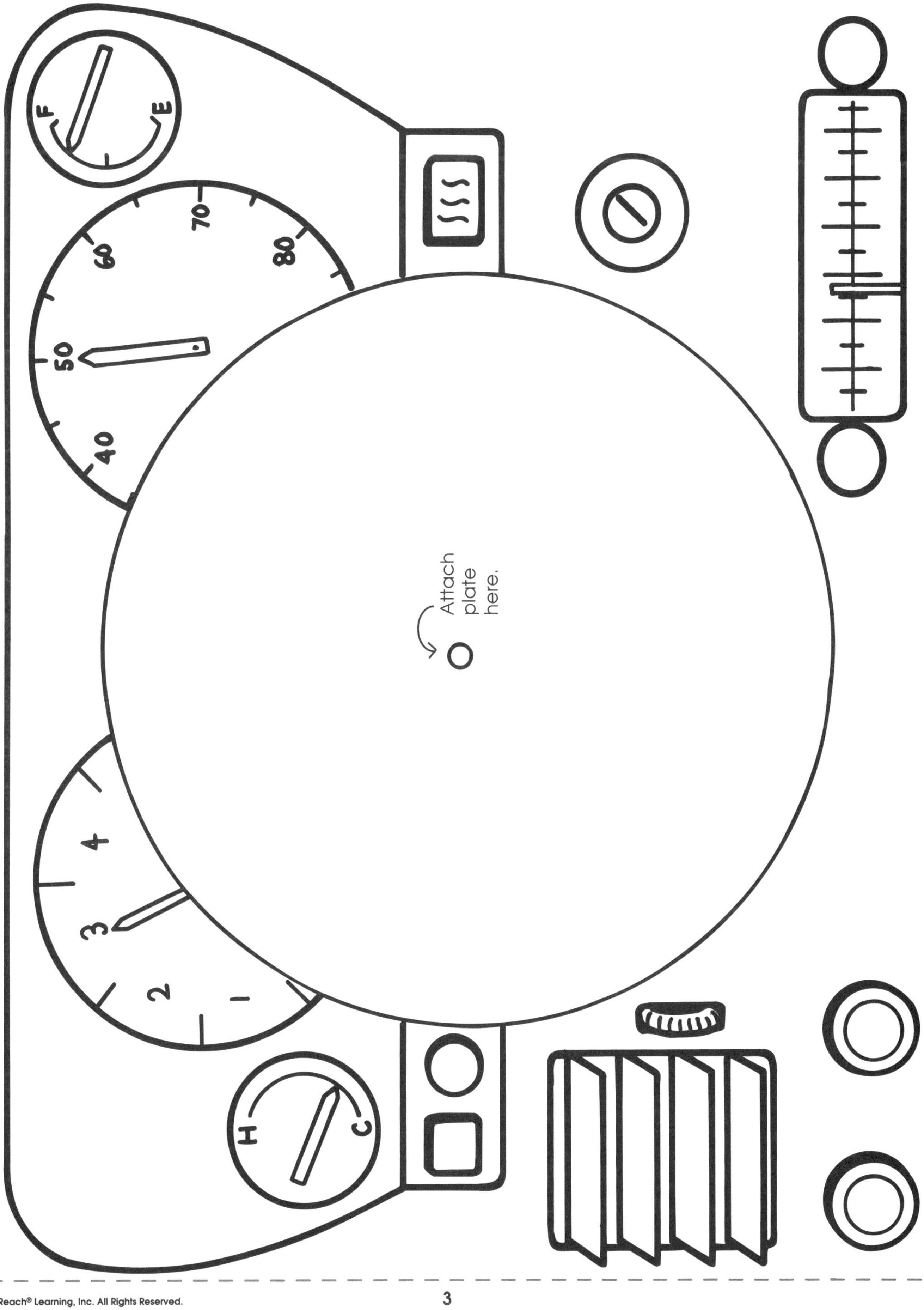

Car Lacing Card

Decorate and mount on cardboard or posterboard. Cut out the car and punch holes around the edge. Tie a long shoelace through one hole. Lace the string in and out of the holes around the car.

Fill 'Er Up

Follow each road to help the cars get to the gas station.

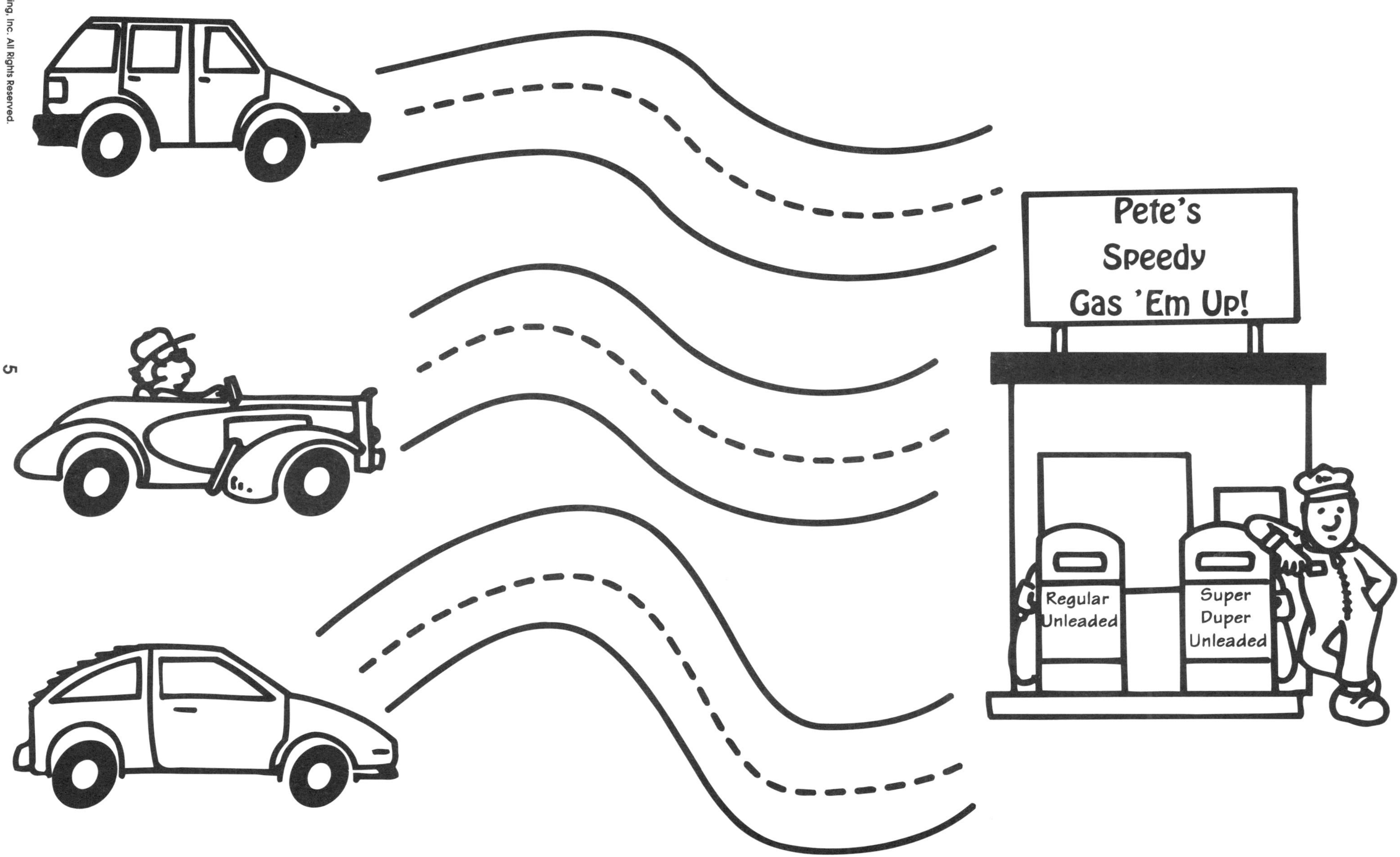

Car Puppet

Cut on dotted line. Decorate both sides of the car and fold where indicated. Tape on the front and bottom, leaving the back open. Slip hand into opening.

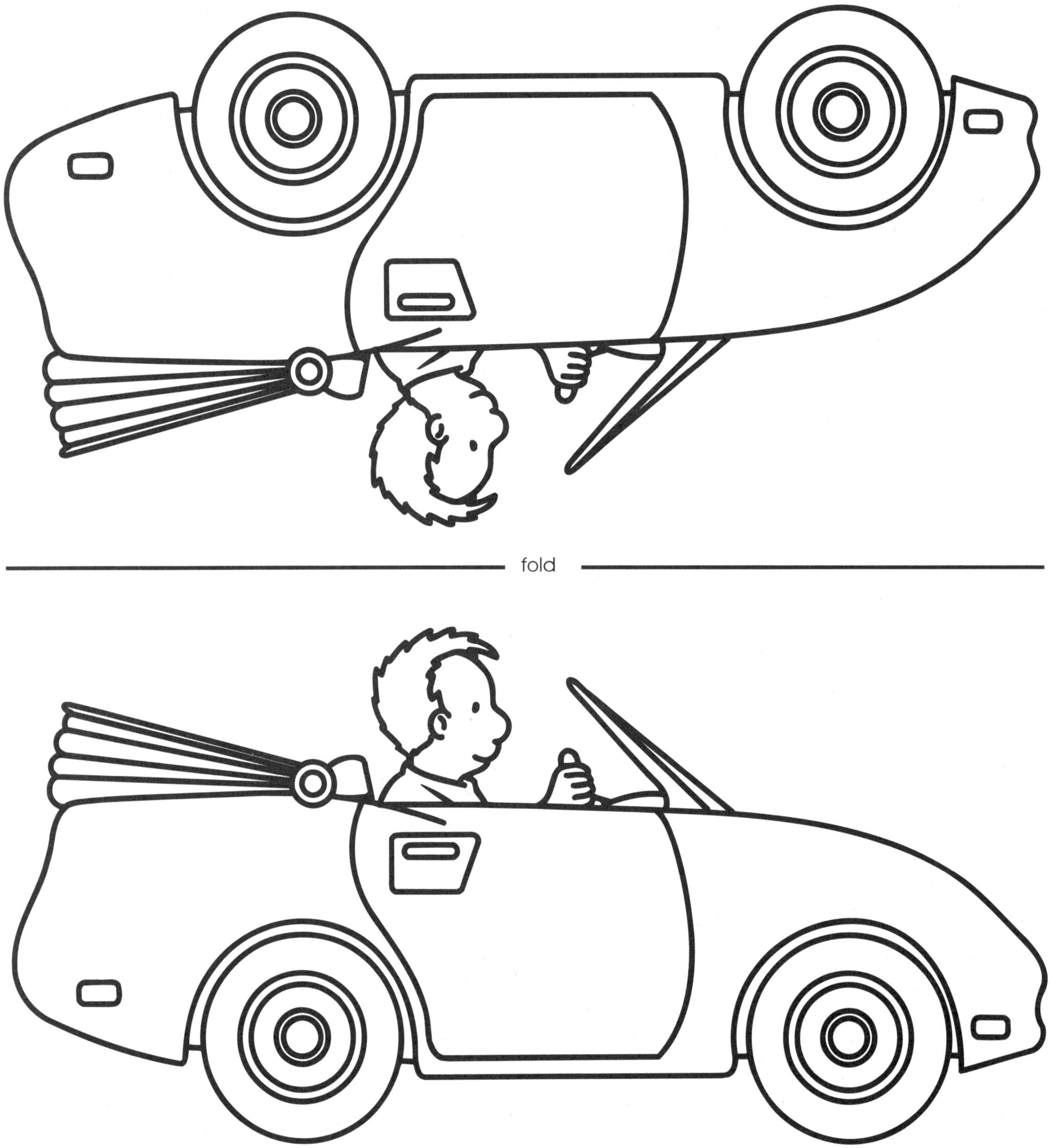

Car Match

Cut on dotted lines and attach each picture beside its match. Decorate as desired.

Find the Wheels

Find the wheels in the picture.
Decorate as desired.

Terrific Trucks

Tractor Trailer Trucks

(tune: "She'll Be Comin' Round the Mountain")

Tractor trailer trucks can carry heavy loads.
Tractor trailer trucks can carry heavy loads.
As they travel to and fro,
On the busy, busy road,
Tractor trailer trucks can carry heavy loads.

Haul Blocks in Trucks

Encourage your child to use a toy tractor trailer truck to haul blocks or other toys.

Tractor Trailer Number Review Game

To make the game:
Create 10 cabs and 10 trailers from construction paper. On each cab, write a number from 1 to 10 and on the trailer draw a series of dots to represent the numbers 1-10.

To play the game:
Help your child identify the number on each truck cab. Ask the child to locate a trailer with corresponding number of dots and place it behind the cab.

The Garbage Truck Picks Up Things For You

(tune: "Twinkle, Twinkle, Little Star")

The garbage truck picks up things for you,
Recyclables and garbage, too!
Bottles, cans, and plastic jugs,
Shoes and fans and even rugs.
The garbage truck picks up things for you,
Recyclables and garbage, too!

What Can a Tractor Trailer Haul?

Encourage your child to dictate all the things that could be hauled in a tractor trailer truck. As your child makes suggestions, print each idea on a sheet of paper. Point to the words as you read the list back to your child. Encourage your child to locate any letters he/she recognizes.

Construction Paper Trucks

Cut a 6" square from construction paper (any color) and several 3" circles from black construction paper. Glue the 6" construction paper square to one end of a 9" x 12" sheet of construction paper. Glue the circles to the base to represent wheels. Decorate the trucks with markers or crayons. For added fun, glue the truck to the side of a box and use the truck to carry small items!

Load a Tractor Trailer

Explore loading boxes into a tractor trailer. Arrange a large cardboard box so that the open end is situated on its side. Then encourage your child to stack or arrange the smaller boxes inside the larger box. Explain that before a tractor trailer leaves with its load, someone has to load the boxes in the back.

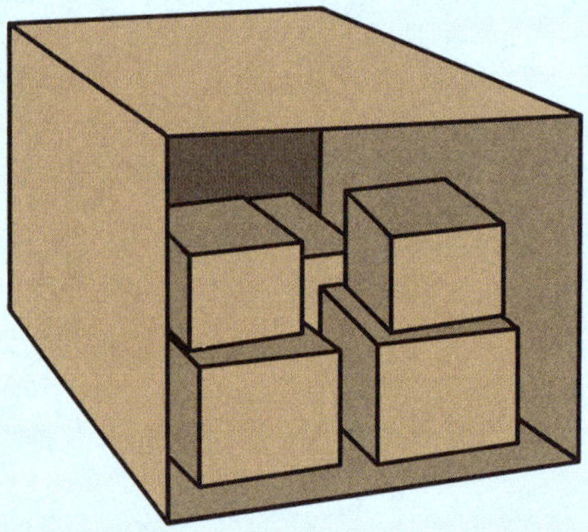

Truck Prop

Decorate pictures and cut along dotted line. Glue to opposite sides of a shoe box.

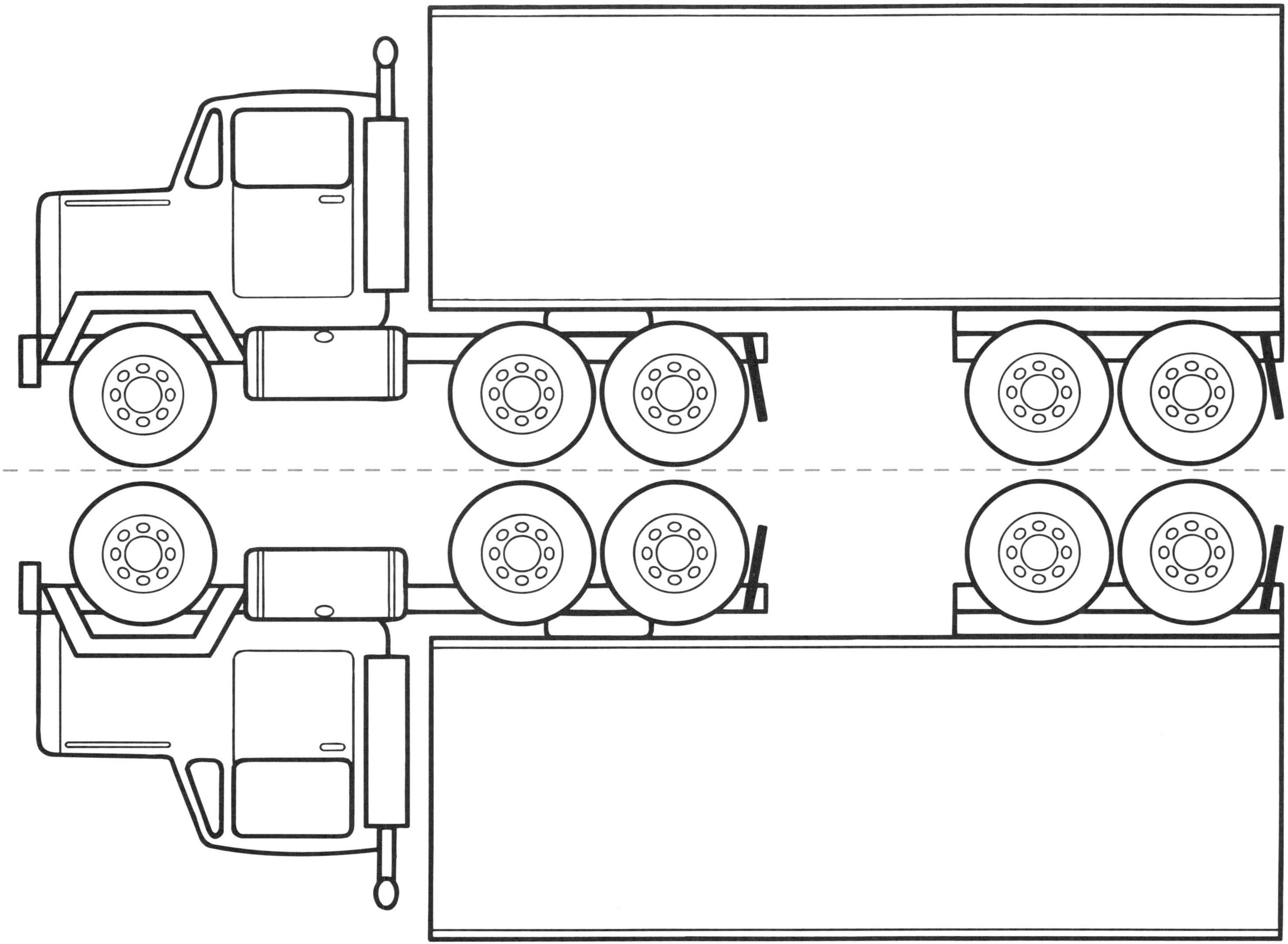

Truck Maze

Find the path through the maze to help the truck get to the store.

Keep On Truckin'

Decorate sheet. Glue pictures to the side of the trailer to show what to haul in the truck.

Help the Trucks Find a Parking Space

Cut on dotted lines. Place each truck in the parking place with the matching number. Decorate as desired.

Garbage Truck Play Set

Decorate the pieces and cut along dotted lines. Attach the garbage truck to one side of a shoe box. Attach the sanitation worker to a toilet-tissue roll. Wrap the garbage can piece around a bathroom-size paper cup.

Truck Mobile

Decorate trucks and cut along dotted lines. Cut a posterboard strip. Attach the ends of the posterboard together to form a ring. Attach two lengths of string to the top of the ring, to be used to hang the mobile. Attach each truck to a strip of paper, and suspend from the posterboard ring

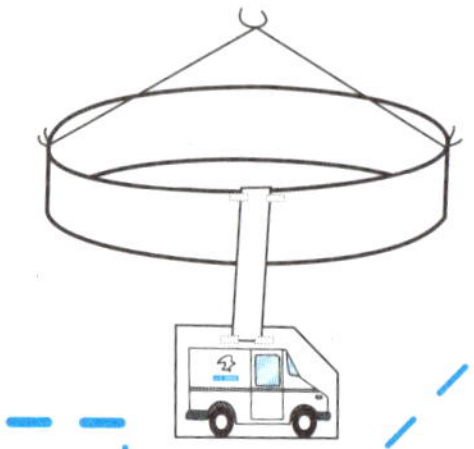

Construction Vehicles

Bulldozer Art

Bulldoze some paint! Place a scoop of thick finger paint on a sheet of finger-paint paper. Give your child a wide craft stick and say, "Pretend you are a bulldozer and this is your blade. Push the blade through the paint." Encourage your child to make engine noises as he/she scrapes the paint across the paper with the stick. Your child might like to try to scrape letters, numbers, or shapes in the paint with the craft stick.

Explore a Pulley

How do pulleys help us? Use this simple activity to help your child find out. Have your child fill a sand bucket with blocks and try to lift it. Ask your child if the bucket is heavy or light. Tie one end of a rope to the sand bucket handle and drape the other end over a doorknob. Then let your child pull the loose end of the rope to lift the bucket. Your child will discover that using the rope makes lifting the bucket easier. Explain that a simple machine called a "pulley" operates in the same way as pulling the rope over the doorknob. Point out that cranes have pulleys that allow them to lift heavy objects easily.

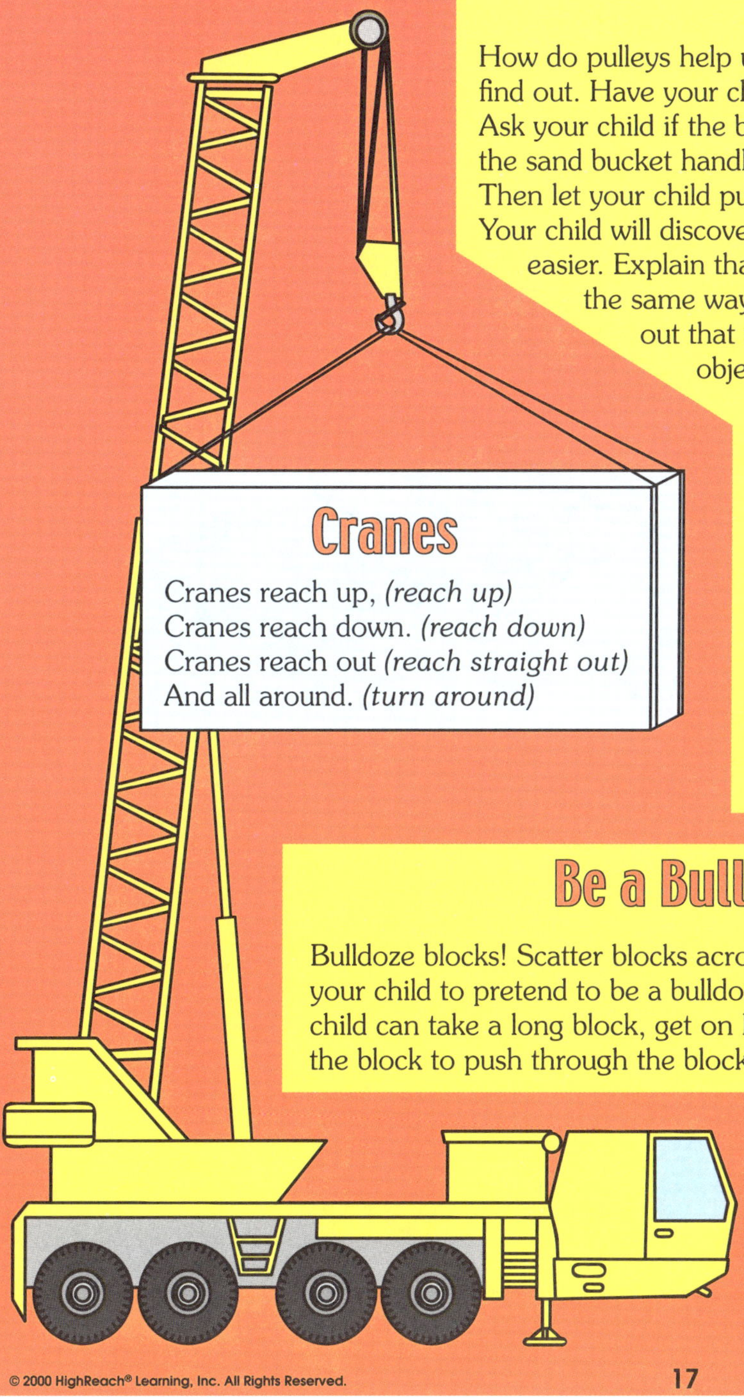

Cranes

Cranes reach up, *(reach up)*
Cranes reach down. *(reach down)*
Cranes reach out *(reach straight out)*
And all around. *(turn around)*

Be a Bulldozer

Bulldoze blocks! Scatter blocks across the floor, then encourage your child to pretend to be a bulldozer and clear the area. Your child can take a long block, get on hands and knees, and use the block to push through the blocks on the floor.

See the Dump Truck

(tune: "Twinkle, Twinkle, Little Star")

See the dump truck going slow.
It must have a great big load,
Full of dirt or maybe rocks.
Working hard, it never stops.
See the dump truck going slow.
It must have a great big load.

Construction Vehicles

The backhoe digs a big, big hole.
The dump truck hauls the dirt.
The grader scrapes the ground so smooth
While all the workers work.

Sand Play

The sandbox is the perfect place to explore construction vehicles. Your child can pick up long sticks or Lincoln Logs® with a crane, move sand around with a dump truck, and make roads in the sand with a bulldozer.

Fill the Dump Truck

Use this game to review colors, shapes, and numbers.

To make this game: Cut shapes from assorted colors of construction paper. Cut ten each of the following shapes: circle, triangle, square, star, and rectangle.

To play the game: Play Fill the Dump Truck. Mix up the shapes and spread them out next to a toy dump truck. Then give your child directions to follow that involve the shapes. For instance, "Please put ten rectangles in the dump truck," or "Please put five red shapes in the dump truck." Help your child count out the corresponding number of rectangles. Once he or she finishes, count the rectangles with your child to make sure the answer is correct. Let him/her dump out the rectangles and then give a new direction to follow.

Serve Snack in a Dump Truck

Place one or more individual bags of granola in the bed of a clean toy dump truck. Drive the truck across the table and let each person dump out a bag. Mmm! The dirt and rocks in that dump truck are tasty!

Construction Vehicle Matching

Cut on dotted lines and attach each vehicle beside its match.

Bulldozer Dot-to-Dot

Connect the dots in order from 1-12 to complete the bulldozer.

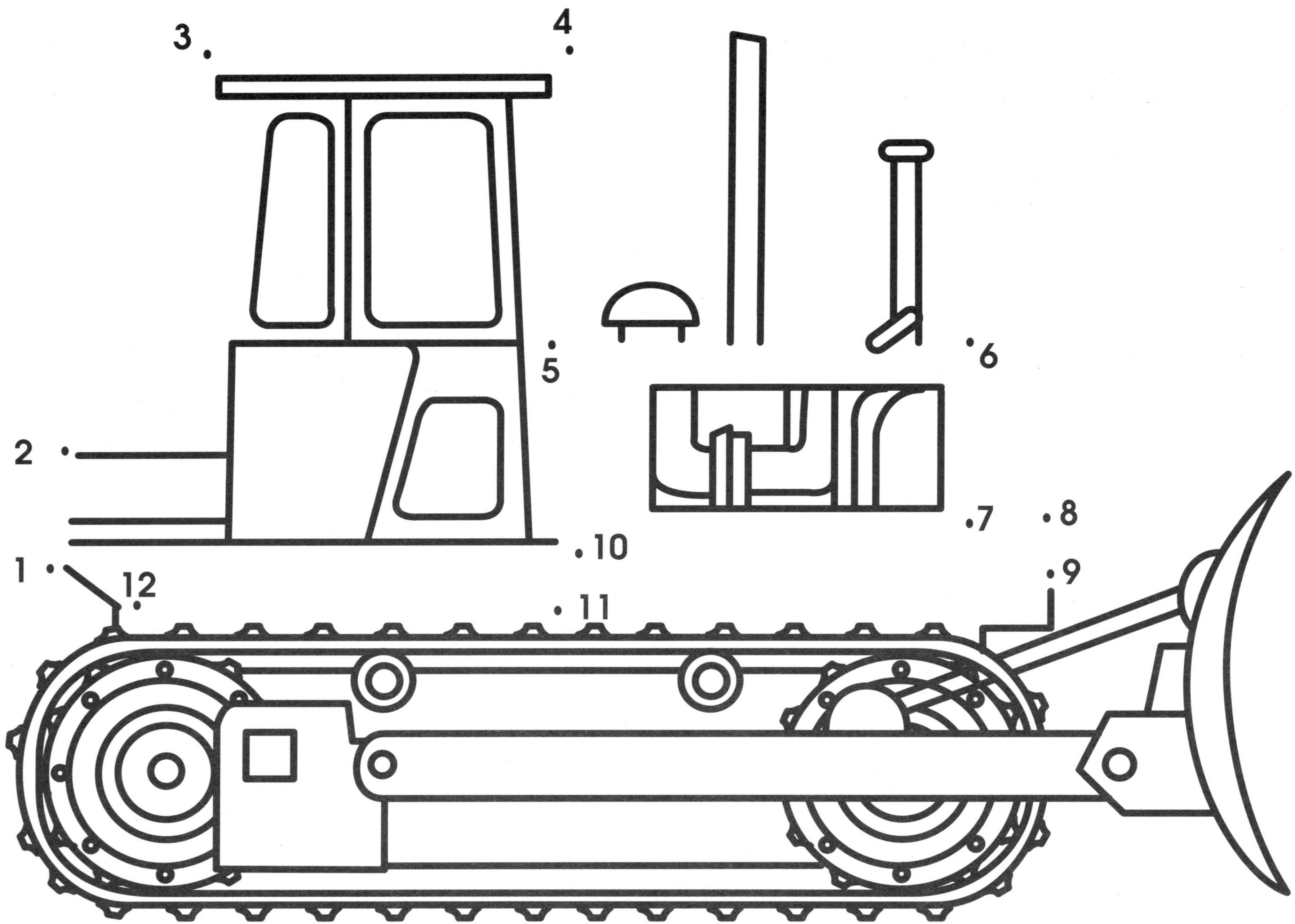

Bulldozer Prop

Decorate both sides of the bulldozer and attach to opposite sides of an empty food box.

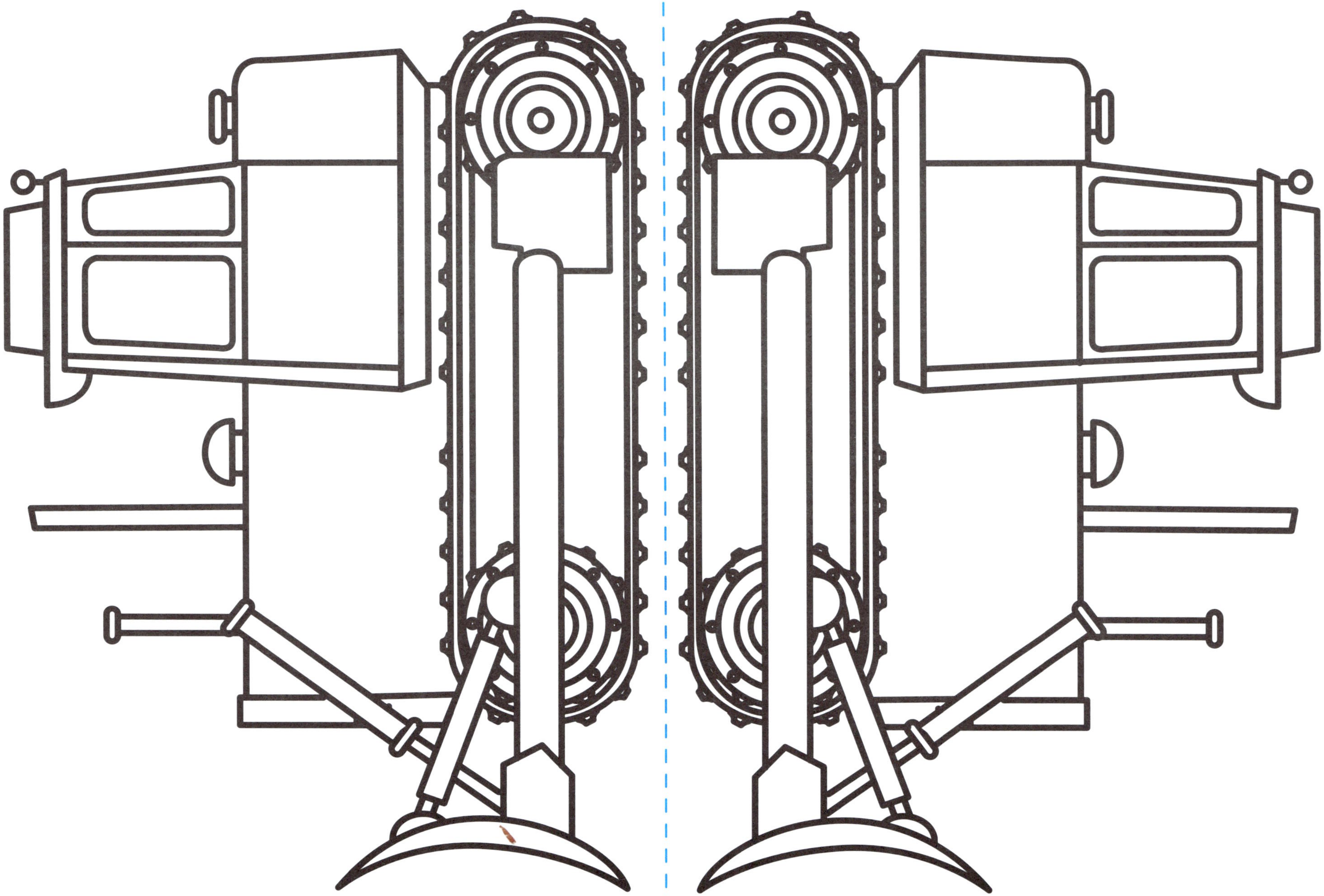

Fill the Truck

Tear pieces of gray construction paper to represent rocks. Add the indicated number of "rocks" to the back of each dump truck.

6

3

9

5

Boats! Boats! And Things That Float!

Create a Sailboat

Provide a plastic container, such as a baked potato dish, a banana split dish, or a lid. Encourage your child to press a small amount of modeling clay into the bottom of the container and insert a drinking straw into the clay to create a mast. Then he/she can use assorted art/collage materials to create a sail and add other details to the boat.

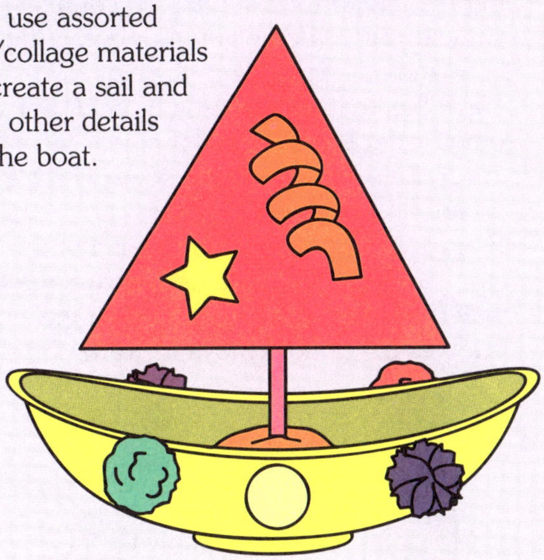

There Are Many Ways to Travel

(tune: "She'll Be Comin' Round the Mountain")

There are many ways to travel here and there.
There are many ways to travel here and there.
You can ride a ship or boat.
There are many things that float.
There are many ways to travel here and there.

Boat Puzzles

Mount pictures of boats on posterboard or cardboard. Cut the pictures into two or more pieces to make puzzles for your child to assemble.

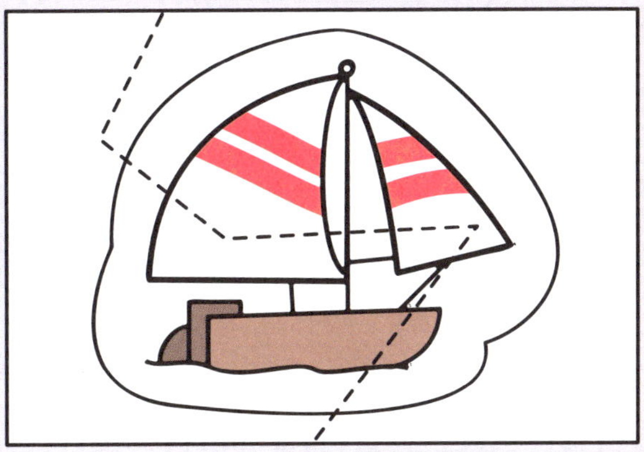

Simple Canoes

Make a paper-towel roll canoe. First, cut a paper-towel roll in half lengthwise. Staple the ends of each half to make canoes. Encourage your child to decorate the canoes with paint or other art materials. Your child may want to put small toy people figures in the canoe and take them for a pretend ride!

Let's Go On a Cruise!

Contact a travel agency in your area and request some brochures or magazines about cruise lines. Look at the brochures with your child and talk about the pictures. Ask your child where he/she would like to travel on a cruise ship.

Explore a Propeller Boat!

These boats make great toys to play with in a bathtub, wading pool, or another water source. Use the illustrations to help you follow the steps below.

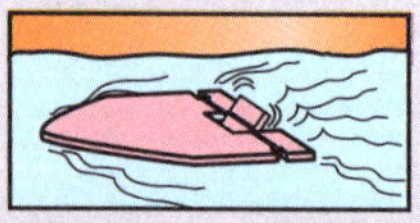

1. Cut a boat shape from a Styrofoam® food tray.
2. Cut a square from the center of the back of the boat and trim the square slightly.
3. Cut a notch on each side of the boat near the back.
4. Slip a rubber band onto the notches so that it fits snugly.
5. Slip the square between the sides of the rubber band and twist.
6. Wind the propeller and hold it in place.
7. Place the boat in the water, and let go of the propeller.
8. Watch the boat zoom across the water!

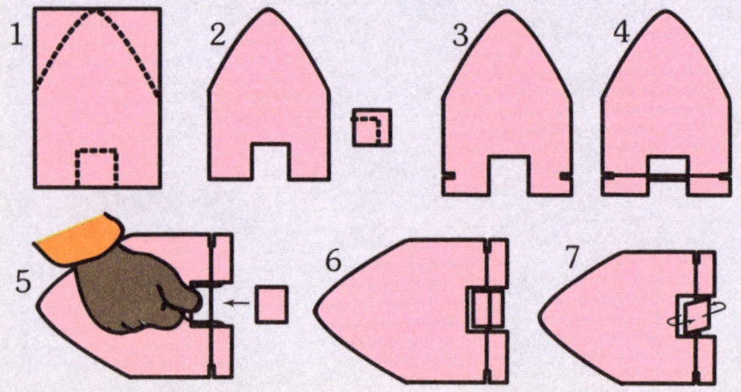

Water-Powered Boat

This boat doesn't need any gas to go – just fill its "tank" with water! Refer to the illustrations as you follow the steps below to assemble the boat.

1. Cut a two-quart milk or juice carton in half lengthwise. You will need one half for each boat you make.
2. Use a hole punch to make a hole in the back of the boat.
3. With a sharp pencil or ice pick, make a hole near the base of a tall plastic cup (adult only).
4. Set the cup in the boat. Insert a drinking straw through the hole in the back of the boat and into the hole in the cup.
5. Place the boat into a bathtub, pool, pond, or other water source. Hold the boat still and cover the open end of the straw with a finger as you fill the cup with water.
6. Remove your finger from the end of the straw and the boat will zoom across the water! As the water pushes out of the straw, it forces the boat to move forward.

Nautical Flags

Show your child the pictures of nautical flags on this page. Encourage your child to use construction paper and art/collage materials to create one or more flags. To make a stick for each flag, roll newspapers tightly and secure with tape.

Hidden Picture

Find the hidden items. Use the key for help.

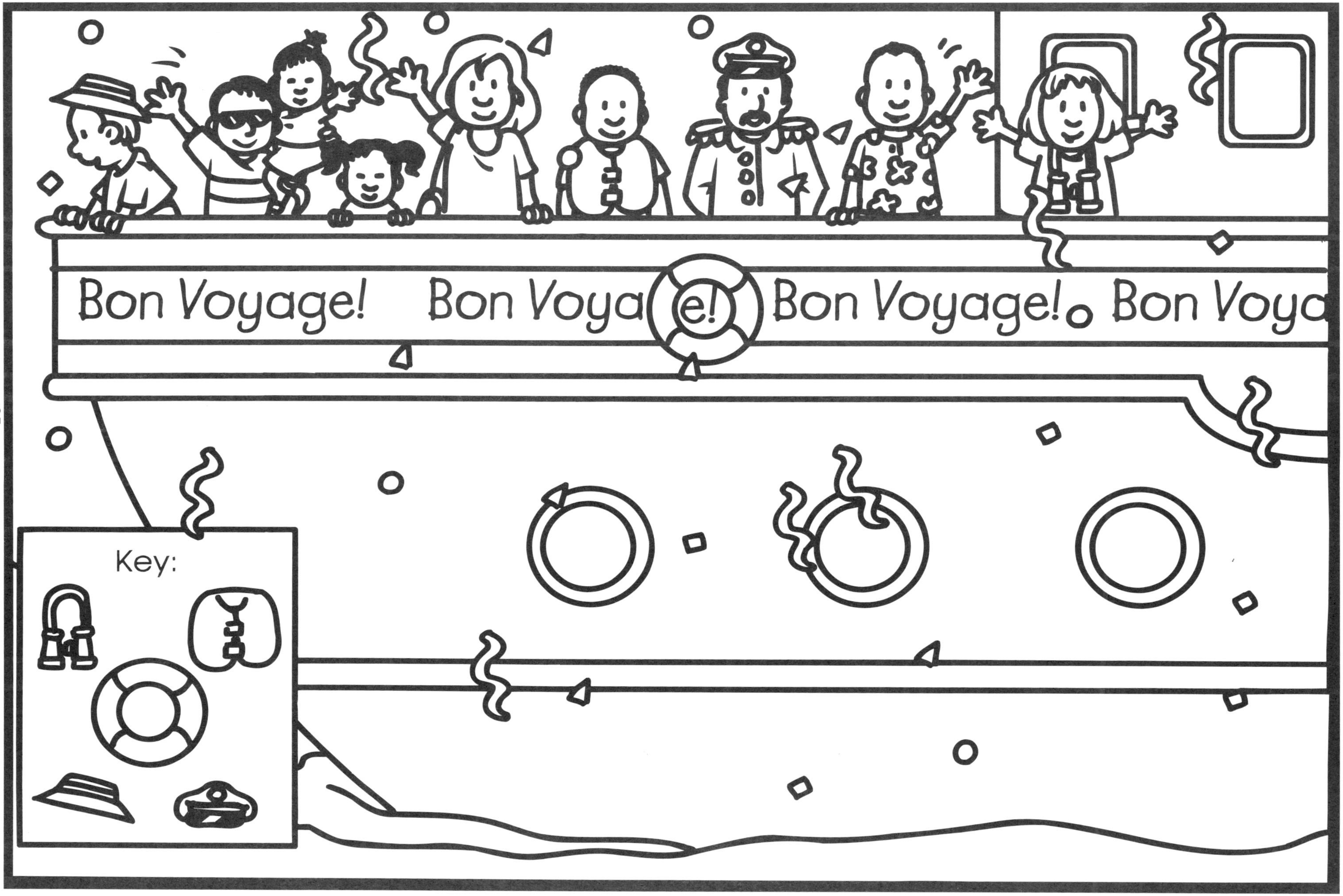

Patterning

Cut on dotted lines. Attach each picture below its match, following the patterns shown.

Motorboat Maze

Find the path through the maze to help the boat get to the dock.

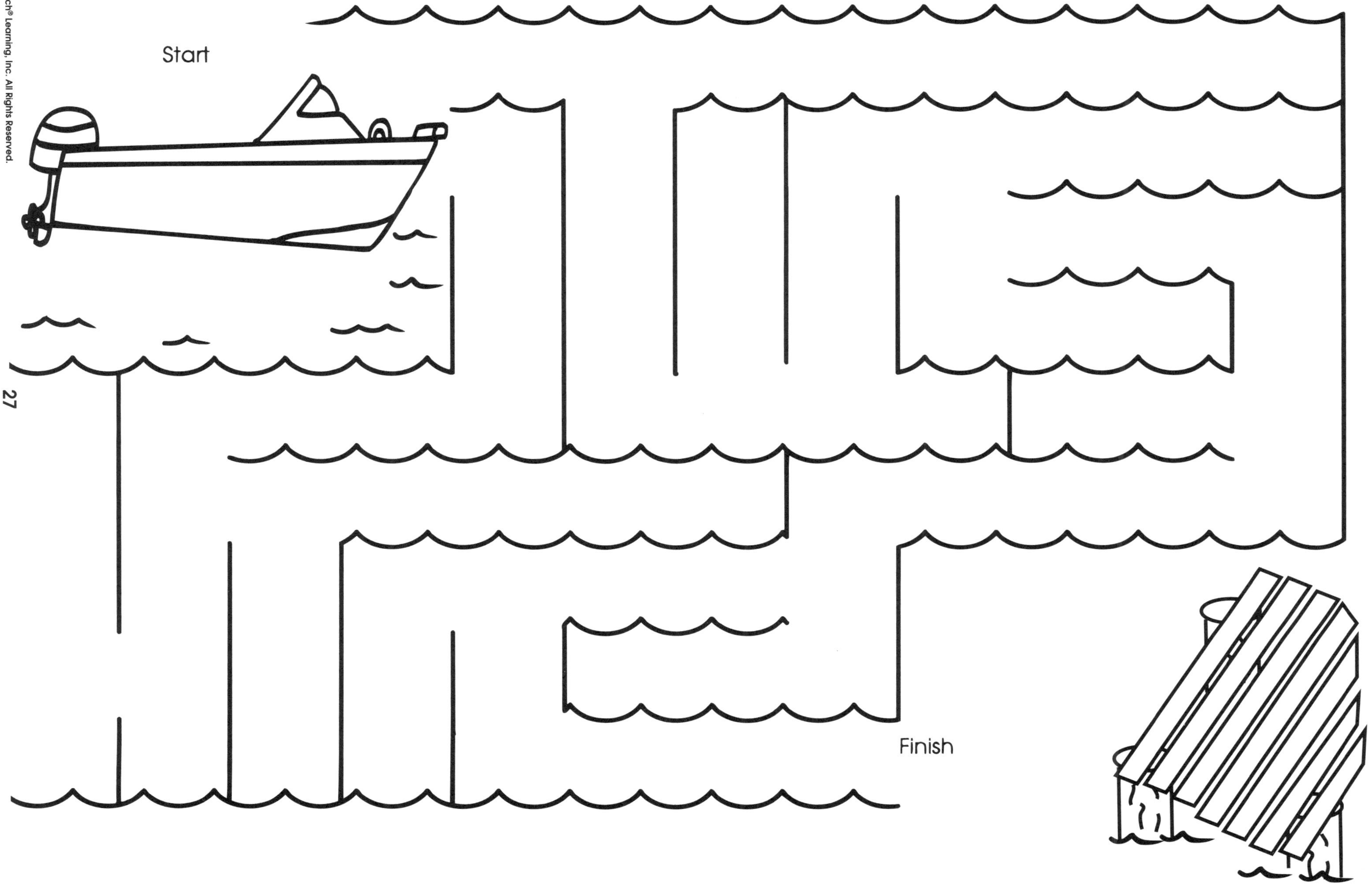

Up! Up! And Away!

Helicopter

(tune: "Yankee Doodle")

Helicopter up and down,
You fly around the city.
Back and forth from here to there,
For you it is so easy.

Helicopter moving fast,
See the rotor spinning.
Flying high above the trees,
For you it is so easy!

Little Airplane in the Sky

(tune: "Twinkle, Twinkle, Little Star")

Little airplane in the sky,
Flying through the clouds so high.
I can see the big wide wings
And hear the propeller sing.
Flying up and flying down,
Bringing people to our town.

Hot Air Balloon

(tune: "Are You Sleeping?")

Hot air balloon,
Hot air balloon,
Floating high,
In the sky.
You are gently floating,
You are gently floating,
In the sky,
In the sky.

Edible Helicopter

This helicopter is good enough to eat! Arrange a scoop of ice cream, $1/2$ banana, and two sugar wafers as shown to create this tasty treat. Eat and enjoy!

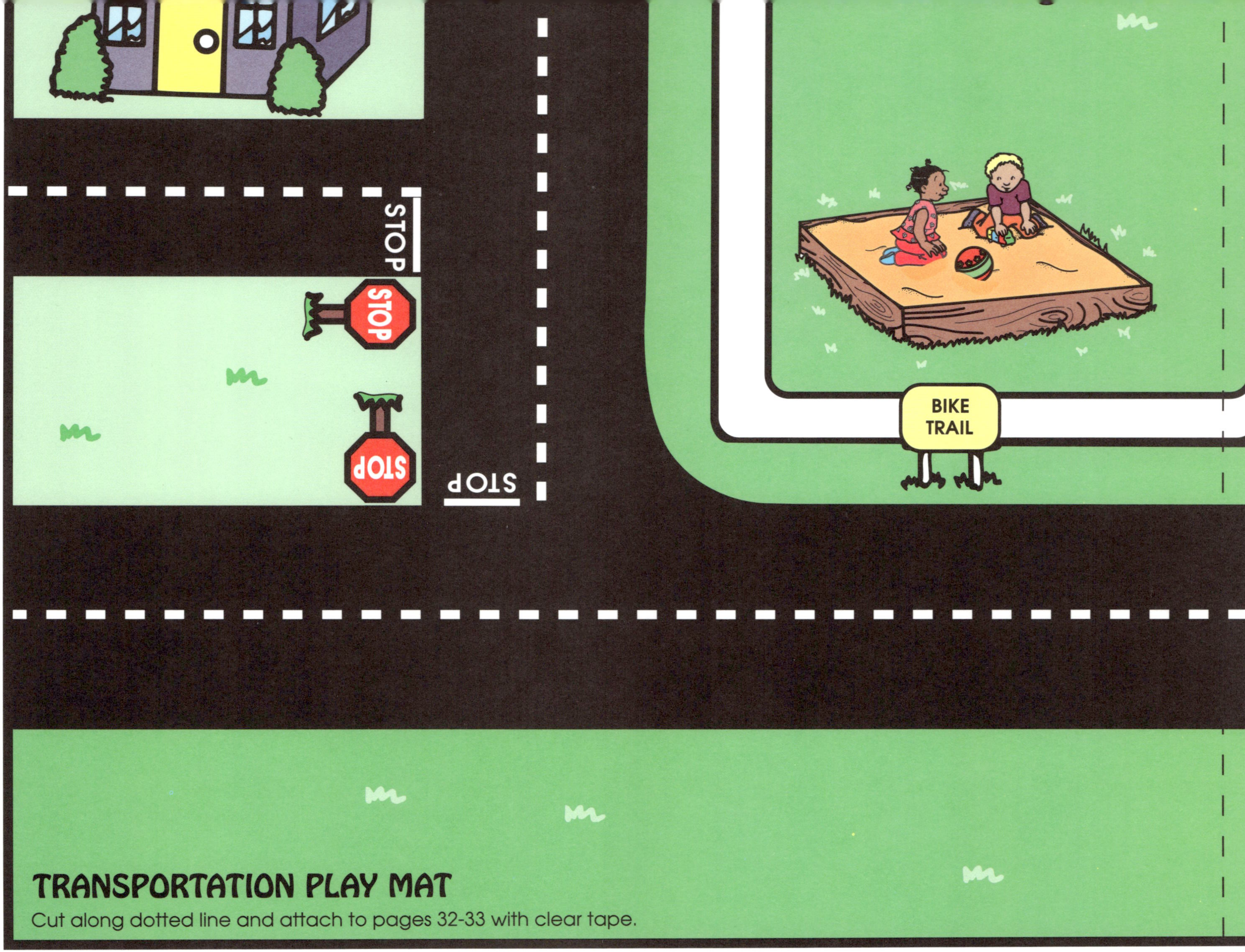

TRANSPORTATION PLAY MAT

Cut along dotted line and attach to pages 32-33 with clear tape.

STOP
STOP
Welcome
to
HighReach
STOP
Airport

STOP
STOP
STOP
STOP
Ed's Gas Station

Hot Air Balloon Craft

Help your child follow the steps below to create this colorful craft.

1. Decorate the outside of two paper/plastic cereal bowls with paint, stickers, or other materials.
2. Cut two equal lengths of yarn and a third piece that is longer.
3. Tape the two equal pieces of yarn about 3" apart on the inside rim of a bowl. Tape the third piece of yarn to the inside rim on the opposite side so that it is centered between the pieces of yarn on the other side.
4. Staple or tape the two decorated bowls together with the yarn between them to create the balloon.
5. To create the basket for the balloon, tape or tie a small bathroom cup to the two pieces of yarn at the bottom.
6. Use the other piece of yarn to hang the balloon from the ceiling.

Watch the Airplanes

If you live near an airport this would be the perfect opportunity to take your child to watch the airplanes take off and land. Your child might also enjoy watching the passengers collect their luggage.

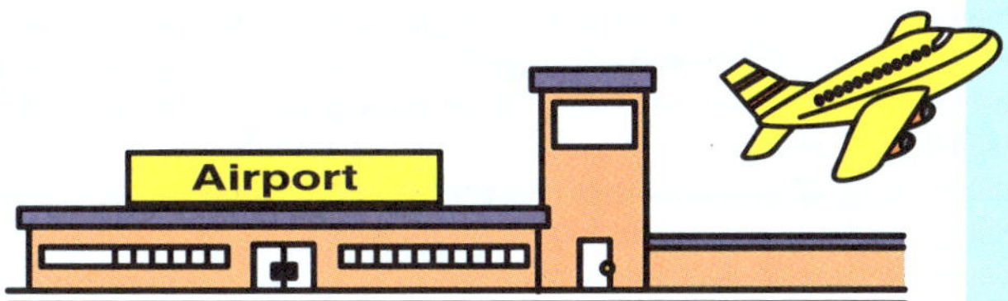

Hot Air Balloon Match Game

To make the game: Cut matching hot air balloons and baskets from wallpaper samples. Mount the baskets side by side on several large sheets of construction paper. Draw lines above each basket to represent ropes.

To play the game: Encourage your child to place each balloon above the matching basket.

Build an Airport

Provide toy airplanes and blocks. Encourage your child to build runways, terminals, and hangars for the airplanes.

Airplane Collage

Encourage your child to decorate the airplanes with assorted markers/crayons and cut out along the dotted lines. Next, cut out the rhyme. Have your child use a sponge to paint a large sheet of paper blue. Help your child to press the pictures and the rhyme into the wet paint. Encourage your child to press cotton balls into the wet paint to represent clouds.

Airplanes

Looking up so high as the clouds go by,
I see pretty airplanes flying in the sky.
I wonder where they're going.
I wonder where they've been.
I wonder if they'll ever fly this way again.

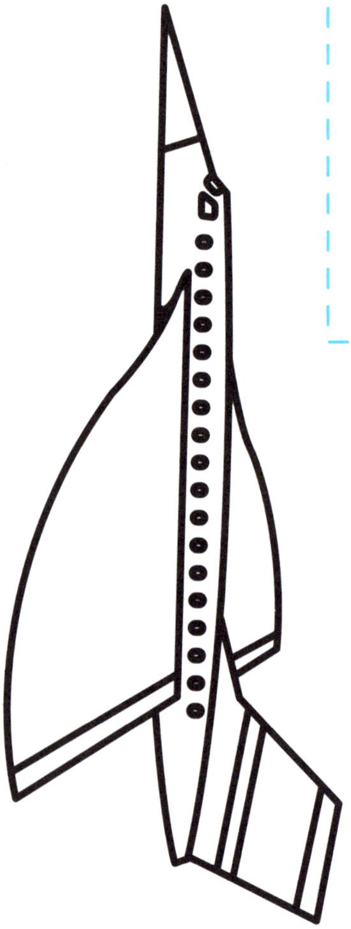

Helicopter Prop

Stuff a small paper lunch bag about half full with old newspapers. Twist the top of the bag and secure with yarn/tape. Decorate the helicopter, cut along dotted lines, and attach to side of bag. Use twisted end as a handle.

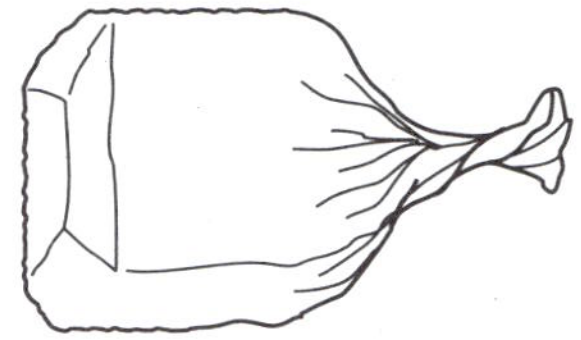

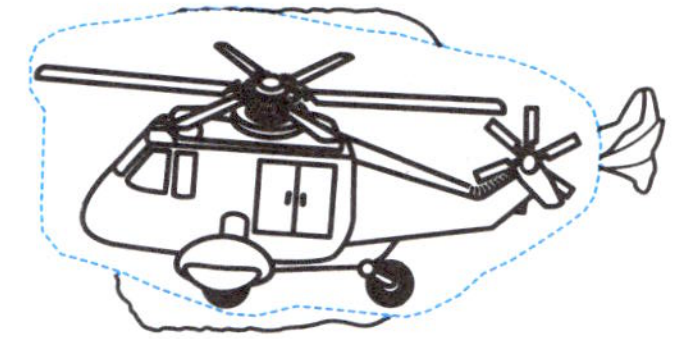

Count the Luggage

Count the luggage. Use the key for help. Write the number beside each.

Choo! Choo!

I'm a Little Train

(tune: "I'm a Little Teapot")

I'm a little train that's puffing down the track.
Hear my wheels sound, clickety clack.
When I see the people, my whistle blows,
"Toot, toot, toot," and off I go!

Traveling Here and There

(tune: "She'll Be Comin' Round the Mountain")

There are many ways to travel here and there.
There are many ways to travel here and there.
Oh, a train moves down the track,
With a clickety, clickety, clack.
There are many ways to travel here and there.

Color Train Game

To make the game: Locate several boxes (e.g., shoe boxes, empty cracker boxes, tissue boxes, etc.). Cover each box with a different color of construction paper. Locate an assortment of items the same color as the boxes you prepared. There will need to be an opening in the top of each box.

To play the game: Show your child the color cars and assorted objects. Place the cars in a line. Then have your child sort the items into the train cars by color. As your child sorts out the objects into the appropriate train car, have him/her name the color of the object.

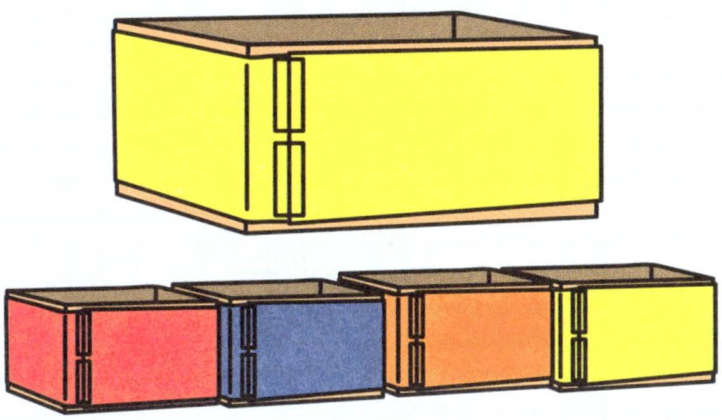

Make Train Tracks

Create pictures of railroad tracks. Have your child glue craft sticks to construction paper to represent railroad ties. Then encourage him/her to glue yarn to the "ties" to make the "rails." As your child creates the railroad track, discuss places it would be fun to go to on a train.

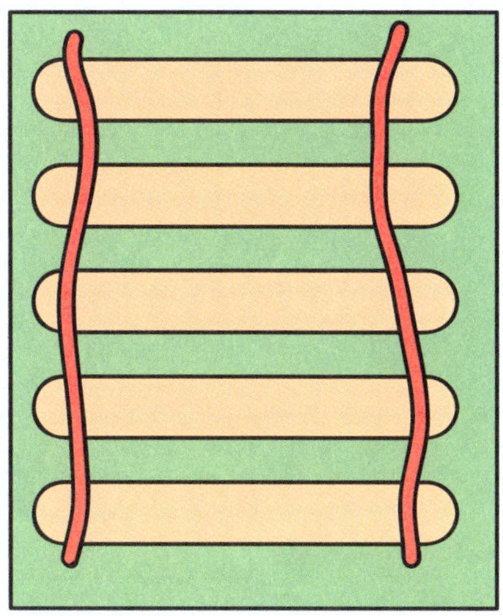

Let's Make a Train!

To make this egg-cellent train, cut a clean empty egg carton in half lengthwise. Next, tape the halves end-to-end with the cup side on top. Put a toilet-tissue roll on one of the end sections to make the train's smokestack. Encourage your child to decorate the train with bits of paper, stickers, or other materials.

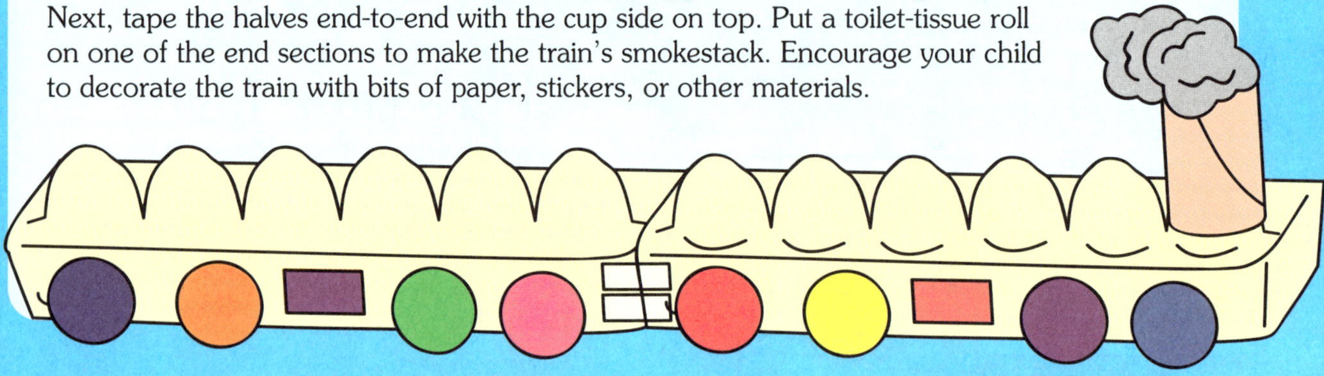

Build a Train Station

Invite your child to use blocks to build a train station and railroad tracks. Provide toy trains for your child to use with the blocks.

Create Train Tickets

Encourage your child to decorate index cards to make train tickets.

Train Reproducible

Use page 43 to make a train. Encourage your child to cut apart the train as indicated by the dotted lines. Attach the train cars in a line on a strip of posterboard. Suggestions for decorating the train are as follows:

- Add smoke to the engine using cotton swabs and black/gray paint.
- Draw any type of freight in the freight car using assorted markers/crayons.
- Attach faces of people to the windows of the passenger car.
- Use a crayon to make the caboose red.

Train Engineer Hat

Pretending to be a train engineer is fun, but it's even more fun with this cute hat. To help your child make the hat, cut the bottom section from a small white paper lunch bag as illustrated. Encourage your child to use blue crayons to make stripes on the white paper bag and half of a small paper plate. When finished, help your child assemble the engineer hat. To do this, cut two 3/4" slits in the paper lunch bag. Fold out the tab and place the half paper plate under the tab. Tape in the front and the back to secure.

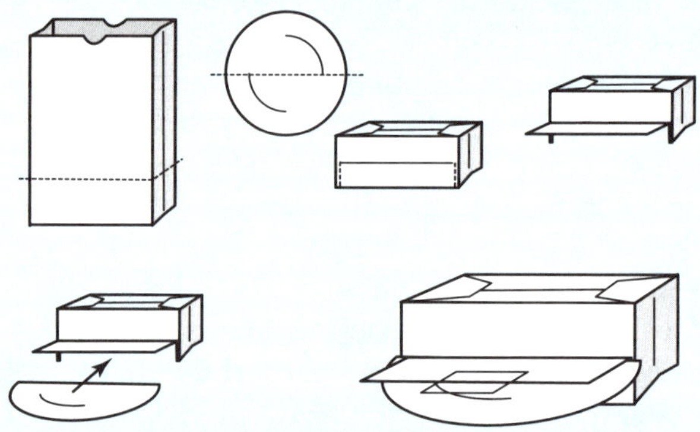

Refer to page 42 for directions.

Here is the engine first in line.

Here is the freight car, right on time.

The passengers ride in a special car.
Let's look in the window and see who they are.

At the end of the train, moving down the track,
Is the little red caboose going clickety-clack.

Train Puppet

Decorate the train. Create a pocket using $1^1/_2$ large paper plates. Attach picture to back of whole paper plate.

back

front

Train Prop

Decorate the train, cut on dotted line, and fold along the center line. Attach to a paper-towel roll as shown.

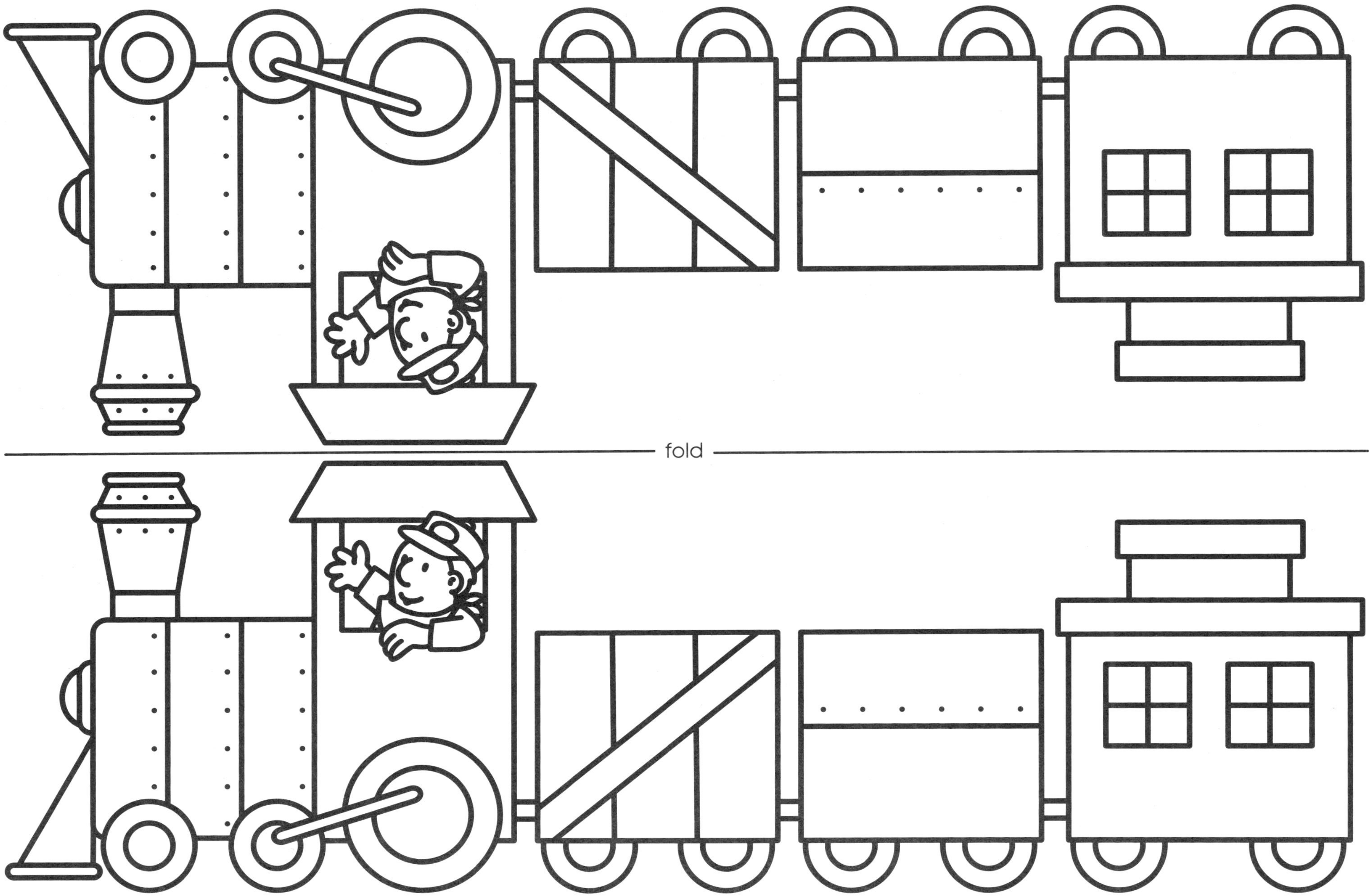

Train Maze

Find the path through the maze to help the train get to the station.

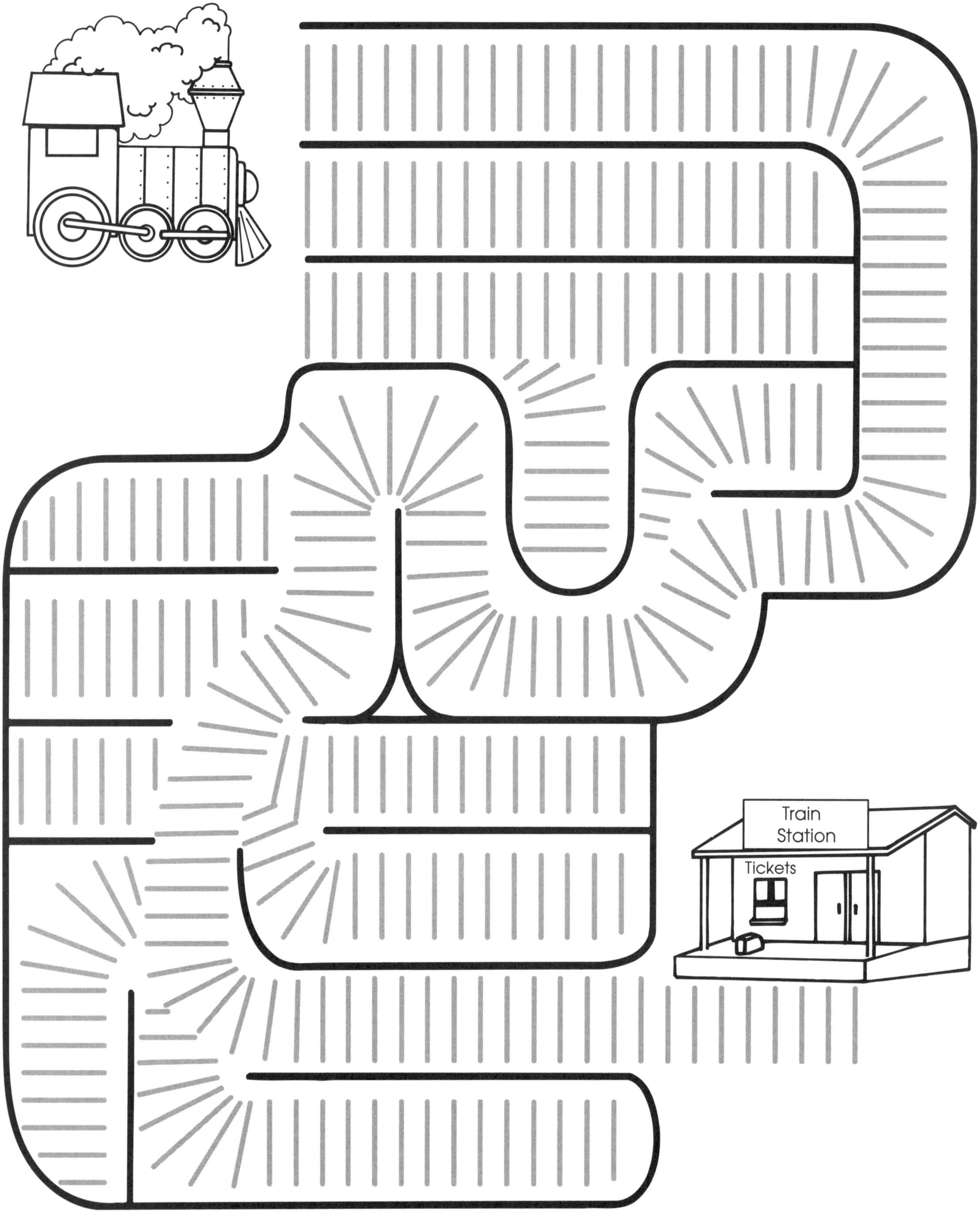

Buses and Taxis

There are Many Kinds of Buses

Talk with your child about different types of buses. A few examples are listed below, but feel free to discuss other buses that would interest your child (church buses, tour buses, etc.).

City buses: These buses travel along regular routes in the city. To ride, you must pay your fare. There are bus stops at various locations in the city where people can get on and off the bus.

School buses: These buses carry children to school and back. Sometimes these buses stop in front of each child's house, but other times a child must walk to a bus stop to meet the bus.

Cross-country buses: These buses carry people from city to city. To ride these buses, the rider must buy a ticket. When it is time to go, the rider usually goes to the bus station to get on the bus.

Stop and Go

(tune: "Mary Had a Little Lamb")

The bus is going down the street,
Down the street, down the street.
The bus is going down the street,
But now it has to STOP!

Role-play a Bus Ride

This activity is fun for any child, but even more fun when a group of friends or family members are gathered. Set up a pretend bus by arranging two rows of chairs, and set an additional chair in the front of one of the rows for the driver's seat. Place a coffee can near the driver's seat. Use plastic lids for bus tokens. Have each rider drop a token into a coffee can when boarding the bus. He/she may also want to role-play the bus driver. Encourage the riders to discuss where the bus is going, what they will do when they arrive, what they will see along the way, and so forth.

Bus Cake

Decorate a loaf cake to resemble a bus. First, let your child use a dull plastic knife to spread frosting on the top and sides of the cake. Give your child round chocolate sandwich cookies and small square cookies. The child can arrange the round cookies along the base of the cake for wheels and attach the square cookies along the sides for windows. If you would like, add details with a tube of decorator icing.

Taxi Cab

(tune: "Twinkle, Twinkle Little Star")

Taxi cab goes down the street.
Hear its horn go, "Beep, beep, beep."
Driving fast and driving slow,
Takes us where we want to go.
Taxi cab goes down the street.
Hear its horn go, "Beep, beep, beep."

Taxi, Taxi

Taxi, taxi, will you stop for me?
Taxi, taxi, will you stop for me?
I have money just for you.
Will you take me to the zoo?
Taxi, taxi, will you stop for me?

Pay the Fare Game

To create the game: Locate an empty margarine tub with a lid. Cut a slit in the center of the lid and snap it onto the margarine tub. Create numbered index cards from 1-10. Provide real coins or large paper cutout coins that will fit through the slit in the top of the margarine tub.

To play the game: Explain to your child that when you take a taxi, you must pay a fare. Show your child the margarine tub, the coins, and the numbered index cards. Place the cards upside down on the table. Encourage your child to choose a card, count out the corresponding number of coins, and place them in the margarine tub to "pay the fare." Take the coins out and continue to play the game in this fashion until all of the numbered index cards have been used.

Book To Share

The Adventures of Taxi Dog by Debra and Sal Barracca
The Wheels on the Bus by Maryann Kovalski
Taxi: A Book of City Words by Betsy and Giulio Maestro
Big Yellow Taxi by Ken Wilson-Max
The Wheels on the Bus by Paul Zelinsky

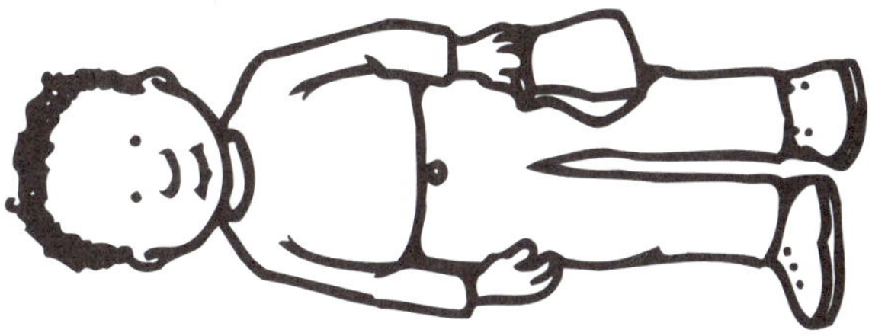

Bus Play Set

Decorate pictures and cut on dotted lines. Attach bus pictures to opposite sides of a toaster-pastry box. Attach each child to 1/2 toilet-tissue roll.

Taxi Match

Cut on dotted lines and attach each taxi beside its match. Decorate as desired.

Maze

Follow the path through the maze to pick up the passengers and take them to see the submarine and sailboat.

Taxi Puzzles

Decorate each picture and cut along dotted lines. Then attach each to a piece of posterboard and cut into several pieces to create a puzzle.

Bus Driver Hat

Cut along dotted lines. Decorate hat and attach to a headband.

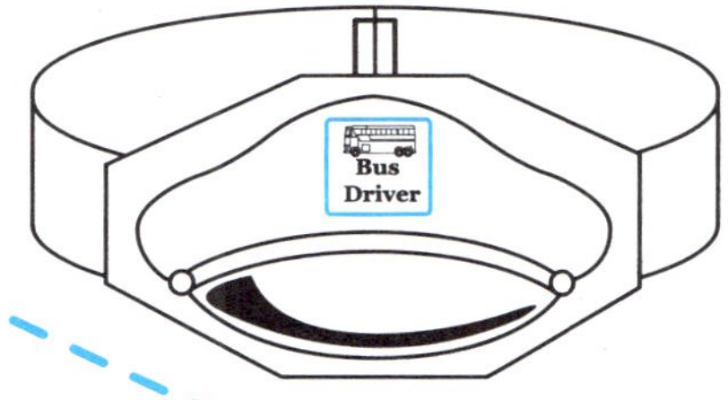

Which Taxi is Different?

In each row put an X on the taxi that is different. Decorate as desired.

Color by Code

Decorate the bus by using the key.

Shape	Color
△	black
♡	red
□	blue
▭	purple
☆	yellow
○	orange

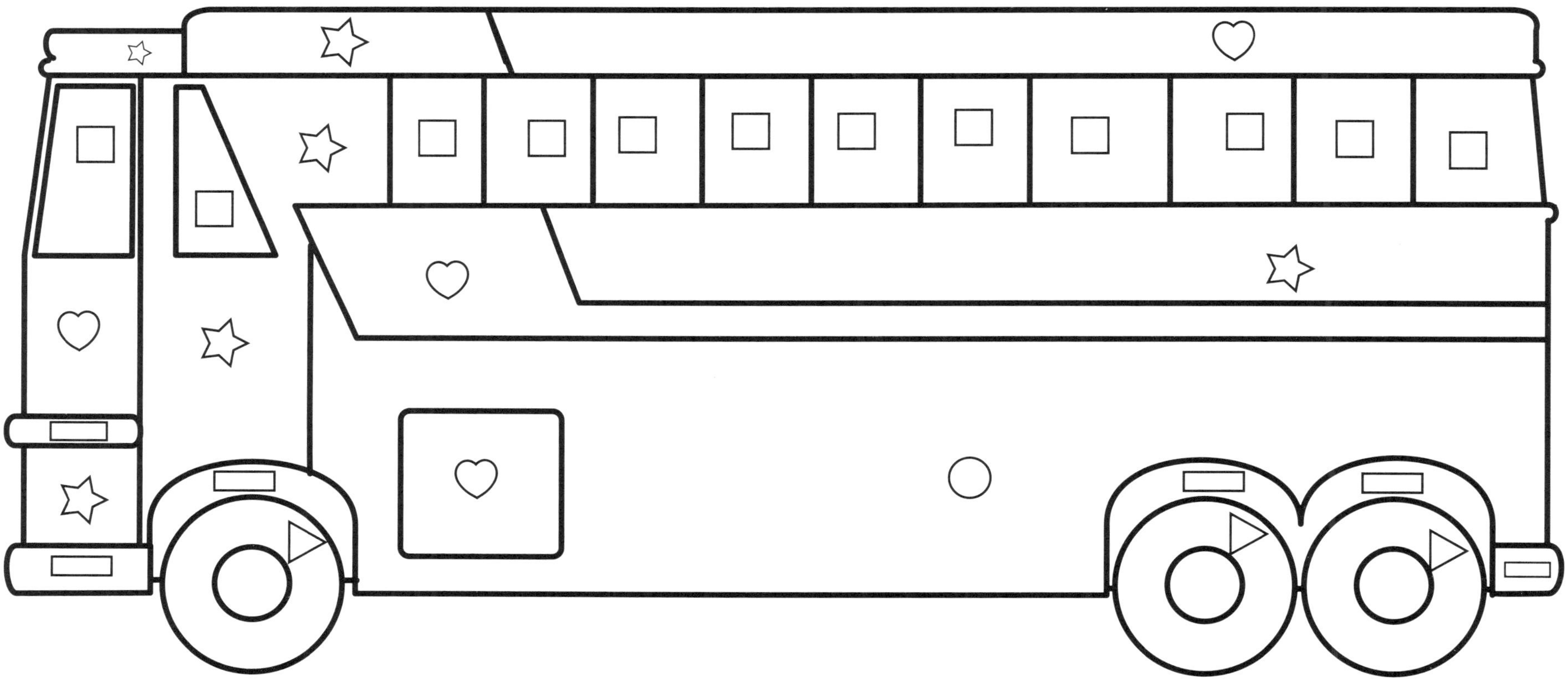

Bridges, Tunnels, and Signs

Edible Traffic Light

Here's a snack that will stop traffic. Have your child spread peanut butter on a graham cracker rectangle and arrange M & M's® candies on it to resemble the lights on a traffic light. As he/she arranges the candies, explain that red means stop, green means go, and yellow means slow down and get ready to stop. Afterwards, your child can enjoy the tasty snack.

Traffic Sign Match-Up Game

To make the game:
Locate two copies of a driver's handbook from your local driver's license office. From the handbooks, cut pairs of traffic sign pictures. Attach each picture to an index card. Mix the cards together.

To play the game:
Encourage your child to sort the cards into matching pairs of traffic signs. After matching the cards, ask your child to identify common ones, such as a stop sign, railroad crossing sign, and others.

Box Tunnel

Learning the opposites over and under is fun with a box tunnel! To make the tunnel, use a sharp knife (adult only) to cut arched openings in opposite sides of a medium-sized cardboard box. Make sure that the openings are large enough for an assortment of toy vehicles to pass through. Encourage your child to roll toy vehicles through the tunnel, or fly airplanes or helicopters over the tunnel. Discuss the opposites over and under as your child plays.

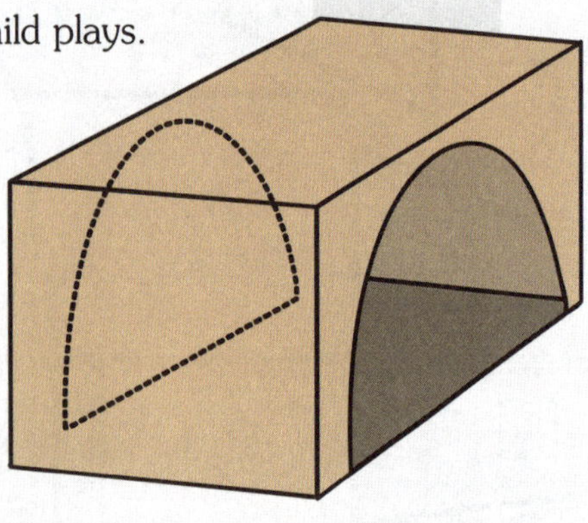

Build Bridges

Encourage your child to build a bridge from blocks and drive toy vehicles across it. Talk with the child about bridges you have crossed when traveling. Explain that bridges are often used when cars need to cross over water.

Traffic Light Book

Decorate as indicated on each page. Cut on dotted lines, stack pages in order, and staple on the left.

Stop at the red light.

Attach a red coding dot to the top position on the traffic light. 1

Go on the green.

Attach a green coding dot to the bottom position on the traffic light. 2

Wait at the yellow.

Attach a yellow coding dot to the center position on the traffic light. 3

That's what the colors mean.

Add all three stickers to the traffic light. 4

Where Does It Belong?

Cut along dotted lines and place each vehicle in the proper place.

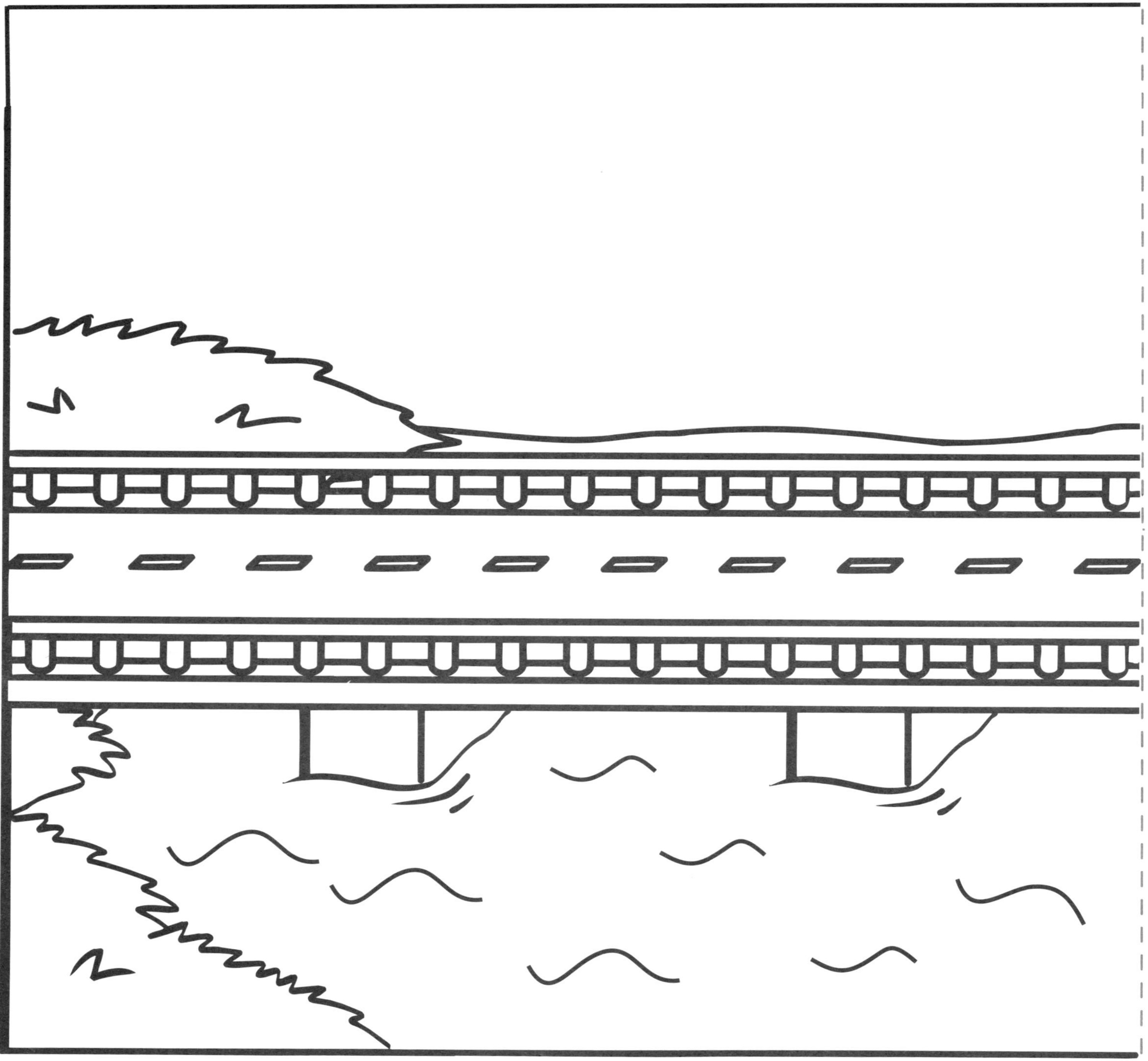

Ordering Sets of Road Signs

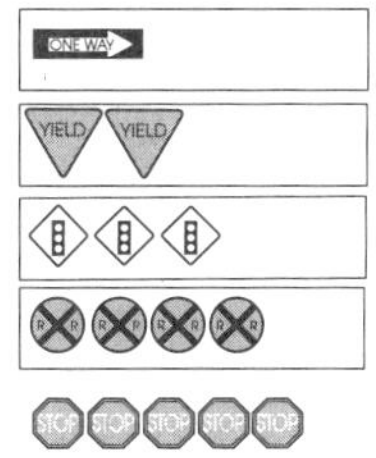

Decorate signs as desired and cut on dotted lines.
Arrange the strips of signs in order from one to five.

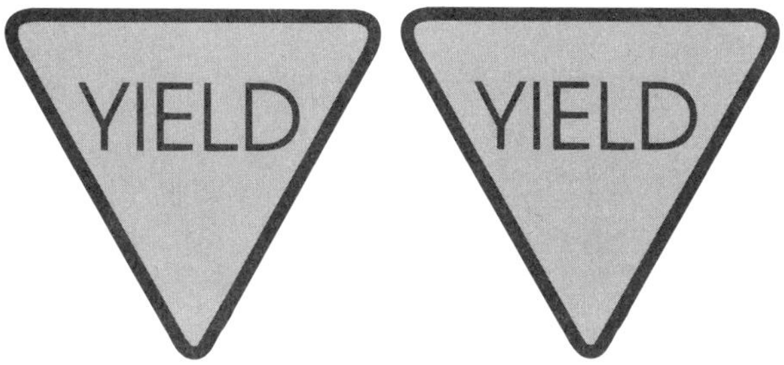

Sign Match

Cut on dotted lines and attach each sign beside its match. Decorate as desired.

Hidden Signs

Find the signs. Use the key for help.

Key:

Stop Sign

Decorate the stop sign and cut along dotted lines. Mount onto a paper plate as shown. Attach a wide craft stick for a handle as shown.

Buckle Up!

Safe Rider Tips

Discuss the following Safe Rider Tips with your child.

- A child who weighs less than 40 pounds should ride in a safety seat.
- A child who weighs more than 40 pounds should use an approved booster seat.
- Keep hands inside car windows.
- Speak quietly, so the driver will not be distracted.
- Keep car doors locked.

Seat Belt Safety

Red light, green light,
Stop and go.
Forward, backward,
To and fro.
When I travel here and there,
Seat belts get me there with care.

Oh, Do You Always Buckle Up?

(tune: "The Muffin Man")

Oh, do you always buckle up,
Buckle up, buckle up?
Oh, do you always buckle up,
It's easy as can be!

Oh, yes, I always buckle up,
Buckle up, buckle up.
Oh, yes, I always buckle up,
It's easy as can be!

Safety Play Set

Decorate each side of van and attach to opposite sides of a small food box. Attach each child to 1/2 toilet-tissue roll.

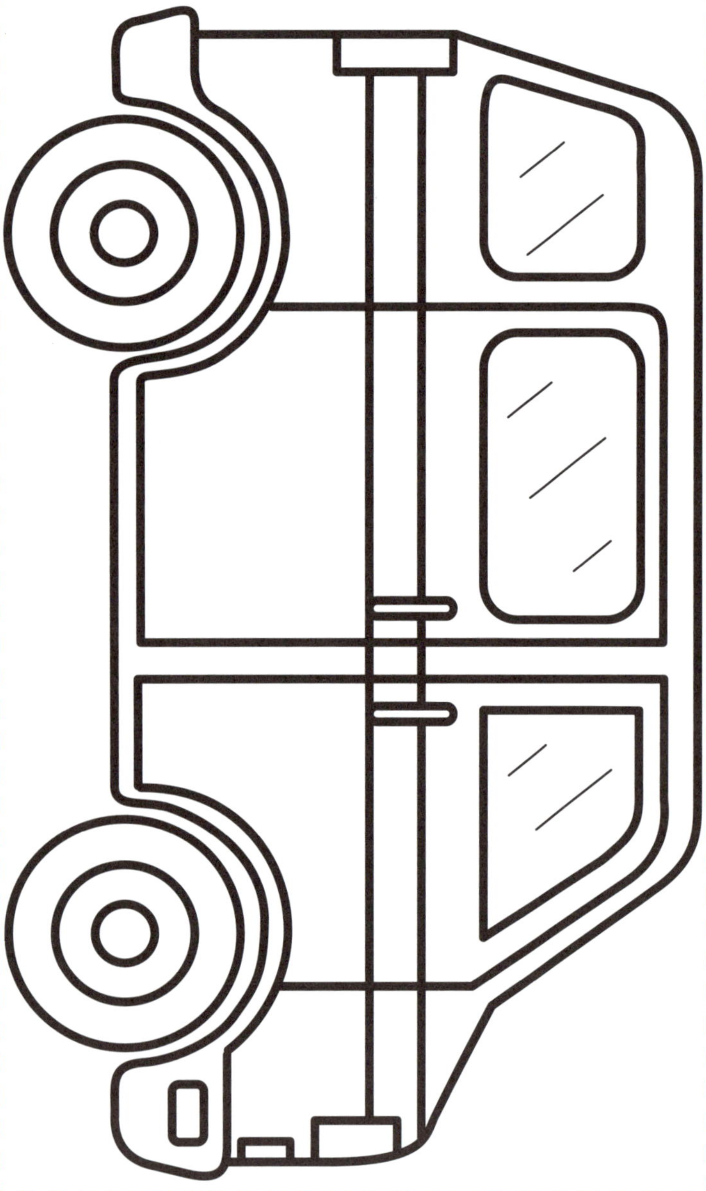

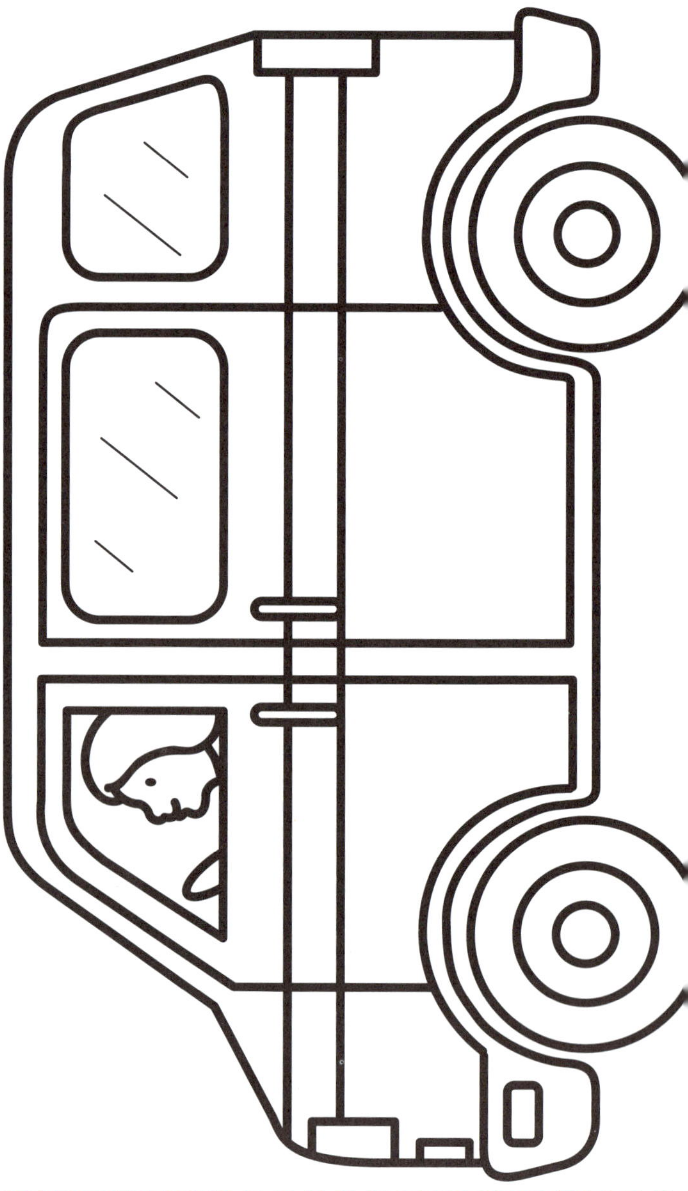